Perfect Gifts

by
Paul McCusker

Perfect Gifts

by
Paul McCusker

Augustine Institute
Greenwood Village, CO

Augustine Institute
6160 S. Syracuse Way, Suite 310
Greenwood Village, CO 80111
Tel: (866) 767-3155
www.augustineinstitute.org

Note: Different versions of some of these stories
have appeared in the *Signs of Grace* series.

Creative Director: Ben Dybas
Cover Design: Lisa Marie Patterson
Illustrations: Robert Dunn

ISBN-978-1-7325247-3-6
Library of Congress Control Number 2018954326

Printed in Canada

Contents

▲▼◄▲▼◄▲▼◄▲▼◄▲▼◄▲▼◄

Introduction   7

1. The Birthday Gifts   9

2. Rules   23

3. Glue   31

4. Stuff   37

5. The Deep End   45

6. Grace   51

7. A Special Place   61

8. A Surprise   71

9. The Car   87

10. Trapped!   95

11. No Escape   105

12. The End Of The Day   115

13. The High Road   125

14. The Low Road   131

15. The Long Road   139

16. Home Again   147

Introduction

▲▼◄▲▼◄▲▼◄▲▼◄▲▼◄▲▼◄

Nicholas and Samantha Perry are twins. Nicholas is often called Nick and Samantha is called Sam. They are seven years old. Very soon they will be eight years old.

They have an older brother named Andrew and an older sister named Lizzy. The name Lizzy is short for Elizabeth. Their parents are named Jon and Belle.

Nick and Sam have a good friend named Brad Wilkes. Brad comes to their house to play. He sometimes leads Nick and Sam into trouble.

Early in the summer the Perry family moved to a town called Hope Springs. Hope Springs is near the Rocky Mountains in Colorado. It is a town that has a lot of fun things to do.

Nick and Sam like Hope Springs. They visited relatives there when they were growing up. Their church is called St. Clare of Assisi Catholic Church. In the fall, Nick and Sam will go to the Catholic school next to the church.

Our stories will tell about Nick's and Sam's life in Hope Springs. Maybe their lives are a lot like yours.

CHAPTER ONE

▲▼◄▲▼◄▲▼◄▲▼◄▲▼◄▲▼◄

The Birthday Gifts

Nick and Sam Perry ran through the woods like the end of summer was chasing them.

And it was.

August had arrived. Summer would be over soon. Every day was one day closer to the start of school.

But first they had a birthday to celebrate. Nick and Sam were twins. Their birthday was August 11th. This coming Saturday!

Sam stopped and bent down onto

her knees to catch her breath. Her dark brown hair was tied back. It fell around her face. She pushed it back.

Nick stopped next to her. "Hurry or he'll get there first," Nick said.

Their friend Brad Wilkes was riding his bike to their house. The twins were on foot. They were racing from the ice cream shop to see who got to the front porch first.

Nick and Sam sprinted onward. They reached the edge of the woods. Their neighborhood was just ahead. They used Mr. Filby's backyard as a shortcut. He was mowing his lawn. He waved to them.

They reached the street and crossed over to their house.

"Did we beat him?" Sam asked.

Just then Brad stepped around the tree in the front yard. "Ha," he said.

Nick groaned. "I would have won if I had a Special Edition High Road mountain bike," he said.

"Maybe you'll get one for your birthday," Brad teased.

The three kids walked into the house and went through to the kitchen. Glasses were pulled from the cupboard. Sam got a pitcher of lemonade from the refrigerator. She poured, and they sat down at the kitchen table.

Nick saw his mom in the back garden. She was digging at the weeds in the flower bed.

"What do you think you'll get for your birthday?" Brad asked.

"I asked for the RetroBlaster game system," Nick said. "I hope they remember."

"How could they forget?" Sam asked. "You've been talking about it for weeks!"

"Maybe you should have asked for the Special Edition High Road mountain bike," said Brad. He took a big gulp of his lemonade.

"I did. My dad said it costs too much. He wants me to save up for it on my own," Nick said.

"What do you want?" Brad asked Sam.

"I want a Polly Playtime Doll with all the extra clothes and the big playhouse," she said.

The two boys rolled their eyes.

"That sounds like a waste of a good birthday gift," Brad said. "My parents always get me things that I need. Clothes and shoes and stuff for school."

Nick looked worried. "What if Mom and Dad give me something I don't want?"

"Maybe they'll give you a Polly Playtime Doll," Brad said with a laugh.

Sam giggled. "I might let you play with my dolls," she said.

Nick frowned. He looked up at the ceiling. His parents' bedroom was right above them. "I'll bet our presents are hidden in their closet."

"How do you know?" Brad asked.

"That's where they always hide them," Nick said.

Sam shook her head. "You know the rule. We're not allowed in there," she said.

Nick stood up and paced around the room. He looked out the large window that faced the backyard. His mom had her back to them as she pulled at the weeds.

"You could sneak up and check," Brad said.

Nick looked at Brad, then at Sam.

"I'll stay here and watch for your mom," said Brad.

It wouldn't hurt anything to have a quick peek, Nick thought. "Come on, Sam," Nick said to his sister.

She looked surprised. "But we're not allowed," she said.

"I just want to see," Nick said. "Don't you want to know? What if you get a boring bracelet or a pair of socks?"

"They've never done that before," Sam said. "They normally get us what we want."

Nick smirked at her. "What about the year you got that play kitchen when you asked for a puppy?" he asked.

Sam pursed her lips.

"Remember how upset you were?" Nick asked.

Sam stood up and looked outside at their mother. "Okay," she said.

The twins dashed from the kitchen and up the stairs. They ran through their parents' bedroom to the closet door and slowly pushed it open. The closet was the walk-in kind. On one side their dad's clothes hung on racks. Their mom's clothes hung on

the other side. The shelves on the far wall were filled with the kinds of boxes and keepsakes grown-ups always seemed to have.

"Where would they hide them?" Sam asked.

Nick took a few steps to the back corner of the closet. Clothes hung down in front of a stack of boxes.

"This is a good hiding place," he said. He pushed the clothes aside.

The flaps of the lid on the top box were slightly open.

Sam stepped up to look.

"Aha!" Nick said. He reached in and pulled out a smaller box. The name Sam was written on the top in their mother's handwriting.

Sam's eyes were wide. She took the box from his hands and opened it up. Inside was a glass figurine of a ballerina. Sam was surprised. The ballerina had been in a display window

at a gift shop downtown. She had told
her mom that she thought it was pretty.

Nick grunted and dug into the box
again. "I see a box for a Polly Playtime
doll in here," he said.

"Really?" Sam said with a little
squeal. "Can I see?"

"We don't have time to take everything
out," Nick said. He rummaged in the

box some more. He thought for sure his parents had forgotten his game. Then he saw a large box at the bottom with the words "RetroBlaster" on the side. "It's here!" he cried out.

Just then they heard a door slam downstairs.

In a loud voice Brad said, "Hi, Mrs. Perry!"

Sam gasped. "It's Mom!"

"Oh no!" Nick said.

Sam reached forward to put the glass ballerina away. Nick spun around to close the box. They bumped into each other.

The ballerina flew out of Sam's hands. It fell onto the carpet. It bounced. Then it hit the bottom of a wooden shelf. There was a small cracking sound. The ballerina broke in two.

The twins put their hands over their mouths to keep from crying out.

"What do we do?" Sam cried out in a whisper.

"We have to put it back in the box!" Nick said.

They could hear their mom and Brad talking downstairs.

Tears filled Sam's eyes as she picked up the two pieces. They put it into the gift box and then the larger box. They ran out of the closet.

When they reached the top of the stairs they saw Brad at the bottom. He said, "I have to go home now."

Nick nodded. "See you later," he said.

Brad walked away.

Sam turned to Nick. "We broke my present!" she whispered.

"Maybe they won't look at it again," Nick said. "They'll wrap it and you can look surprised when you open it up."

"But we broke it!" Sam said. Her eyes were wide.

Nick felt sick. "I'm going to my room," he said.

New tears came to Sam's eyes. She ran to her bedroom.

Nick heard his mom come up the stairs.

"I'm going to wash up," she called out. He heard her footsteps fade down the hall as she went into her bedroom. After a few minutes, he heard the water running in the shower.

Sam came to Nick's doorway. She wiped her eyes. "Mom will know," she said.

"How?" he asked. "We put everything back."

"Are you sure?" Sam asked.

Nick wondered. Had they? Did he close the big box? Did he move his dad's clothes back in front of it?

The next ten minutes were painful.

They listened together as the shower stopped. They imagined their mom getting dressed in the closet. They wondered if she would know they had sneaked in.

"She won't know," Nick said to Sam.

They heard their mom come out into the hall. "Nicholas! Samantha! Where are you?" she called out.

They knew that tone of voice. The twins froze where they were.

Their mom appeared in Nick's doorway. In her hands was the broken ballerina.

Chapter Two

▲▼◀▲▼◀▲▼◀▲▼◀▲▼◀▲▼◀

Rules

Nick and Sam weren't very happy. They sat at the kitchen table while their mom made dinner for later that evening. The summer sun came through the back window. Kids laughed and screeched from the swing set next door. They should be outside playing now. Instead they were in trouble.

In front of them sat the two pieces of broken ballerina.

Belle, their mom, stirred something in a large bowl. It made a loud *ratta-*

tat-tat sound. "You broke the rule," she said. "You disobeyed your father and me. What should I do?"

Sam hung her head. "I don't know," she said softly.

"Your birthday is in a couple of days," their mother said. "Why couldn't you wait a couple of days?"

"I was afraid you might not get me what I wanted," Nick said. He reached out to touch the broken ballerina. Sam frowned at him. He pulled his hand back.

Their mother put the bowl down. "Some parents wouldn't give you those presents because of what you did," she said.

Nick and Sam looked at their mother. They were alarmed.

"I'll have to talk to your father about this," their mother said. She turned and put a large pan into the oven. "Until then, you will both do a few extra chores."

Nick put his head in his hands.

"Sam, I want you to tidy up your bathroom," Mrs. Perry said. "Nick, I want you to sweep the kitchen floor."

"That's not so bad," Sam said quietly.

"That's only the start," their mother said. She walked out of the kitchen.

Sam nudged the broken ballerina pieces with her finger. "I hope we can glue it," she said.

Nick wondered if his parents would take the RetroBlaster game back to the store. What if they really decided not to give it to him? That would be the worst birthday ever.

Sam went off to do her chore. Nick went to the pantry and got out the broom and dustpan. He began to sweep the floor. He hated sweeping the floor.

A few minutes later his older brother Andrew came into the kitchen. Andrew was twelve years old. He went to the counter and took bread from the breadbox to make a sandwich.

"Mom just put dinner in the oven," Nick said.

Andrew looked up at the clock on the wall. "That's three hours from now," he said and went to the pantry. He grabbed a jar of peanut butter. "Why are you sweeping the floor?" he asked.

Nick told him what happened.

Andrew smiled and pointed to a corner of the kitchen floor. "You missed a spot," he teased.

"I don't know why it's such a big deal," Nick growled. "Who cares if you see your presents before you get them?"

Andrew took a knife from the silverware drawer. He began to spread peanut butter on the bread. "You know the rules. Their closet is off-limits. You broke the rule and now you're being punished."

Nick stopped sweeping. "I don't like all these rules. You have to do this or you can't do that. What's the point?"

Andrew looked at his little brother. "Do you think it would be better if there weren't any rules?"

"Yeah," Nick said. He thought it would be *great* if he didn't have to follow any rules.

"Okay. Let's pretend there are no rules." Andrew picked up a piece of bread. He tore it into pieces and dropped the crumbs on the floor.

"Hey!" Nick shouted. "I just swept that!"

"So?" Andrew said. "There are no rules. I can drop crumbs on the floor if I want."

"It's a waste of food," Nick said.

"Says who? If there are no rules

then I can waste food," Andrew said. "I can pick up the trash can and dump it on your head. I can grab the car keys and drive the car down the sidewalk."

"You can't do that," Nick said. "You'll get arrested."

Andrew shook his head. He said, "No rules, no laws. The police can't arrest me. Everybody can do whatever they want when they want to. I can walk upstairs and take your favorite games from your room if I want. Maybe I'll throw your bed out the window."

"That's crazy," Nick said.

"It sure is," Andrew said as he picked up his sandwich and walked out.

"Hey, come back here!" Nick shouted. "You have to clean up these crumbs!"

Andrew called back from the other

room. "There are no rules, so I don't have to."

Nick looked down at the scattered crumbs. He didn't like not having rules.

CHAPTER THREE

▲▼◀▲▼◀▲▼◀▲▼◀▲▼◀▲▼◀

Glue

Sam sat at the kitchen table with her mother. She watched as her mom carefully glued the two pieces of the broken ballerina back together.

"It's a good thing she didn't shatter," her mom said. "I don't think I could fix her if she had broken into small pieces."

Sam could still see the ballerina fall from her hands. It bounced on the carpet of her parents' closet. Then it broke against the bottom of a wooden shelf.

"Your dad and I don't create rules to be mean," her mom said. "Rules are there to help you, to keep you safe."

Sam kept her eyes fixed on the ballerina. She wanted to say that it was Brad's idea. She wanted to blame Nick. But she didn't. She knew it was her fault too.

Her mom said, "Sometimes we make rules because we know things that you don't know. Sometimes the rules are there to teach you."

Sam thought for a moment. Then she asked, "What does the rule about looking in your closet teach us?"

"That's a very good question," her mom said. "Why do you think we have that rule?"

"To teach us not to be nosy?" Sam asked.

Her mom smiled at her.

"To be patient?" Sam added.

Her mom leaned back in her chair. "The rule can teach you those things," she said. "The rule also teaches you to respect other people's boundaries. The closet is *our* closet, not yours. What we keep in there is *ours*, not yours."

She felt her mom's hand gently rest on hers.

"You have to trust us," her mom said. "You need to have faith that we love you and want what's best for you."

Sam looked at the ballerina again. She wondered if the glue would hold it together.

Her mom said, "When you break the rules you break other things."

Sam gazed up at her. "Like what?" she asked.

"Our relationship," her mom said and took her hand away.

Sam frowned. "What do you mean?"

"Relationships are based on trust. When you break our rules you show that you don't trust us," her mom said. "You also show that we can't trust you."

Sam felt bad. She hadn't thought that breaking a rule would hurt them.

Her mom continued, "We love you. And forgiveness is part of that love. We want you to trust us, and we want to trust you."

"I'm sorry," Sam said softly.

"Saying you're sorry is okay for accidents," her mom said. "When you do something on purpose, it's better to ask, 'Will you forgive me?'"

Sam swallowed hard. Then she looked at her mom and asked, "Will you forgive me?"

"Of course I do." Her mom lightly touched Sam's hair.

Sam thought she might cry again.

Her mom gestured to the ballerina. "Forgiveness is like the glue that helps fix what was broken," she said.

Sam leaned close to the ballerina. "But I can still see where I broke it," she said.

Her mother carefully picked up the ballerina. "Once a broken relationship is fixed, you can still see the cracks," she said. "There will always be marks. Sometimes those marks help us remember what happened. It reminds us to be careful and not to do what we did to break things."

Sam sat up and looked at the ballerina in her mom's hands.

"Sometimes the relationship isn't what it was before," her mom added. "But it can still be beautiful."

Like her, Sam thought.

CHAPTER FOUR

▲▼◀▲▼◀▲▼◀▲▼◀▲▼◀▲▼◀

Stuff

It's not fair, Nick thought.

He was cleaning his room. Extra chores were part of his punishment for sneaking into his parents' closet.

All I did was look at my birthday present, he thought.

He picked up a black sock and looked around. He didn't know where the other sock was. He didn't know what to do with it so he shoved the sock into the top drawer of his dresser next to a half-eaten candy bar.

It's a stupid rule, Nick thought. *What's wrong with seeing my birthday present before my birthday?*

Nick picked up the candy bar. He wondered if it was still good to eat. There were bits of fuzz stuck to the chocolate. He put the candy bar back in the drawer.

Someone should make a rule that you can't get in trouble a week before your birthday, he thought.

He stood in the middle of his room and scowled. What if his parents decided to teach him a lesson? What if they didn't give him the RetroBlaster game for his birthday?

Nick kicked at a baseball glove lying next to his bed. A baseball fell out and rolled under his bed.

I should say I'm sorry, he thought. *If I say I'm sorry then they have to give me the game.*

He looked at a small statue of Saint

Francis on his dresser. The eyes of the statue were looking at him. He felt a pang of guilt. *It would be wrong to say I'm sorry just to get the game*, he thought.

"Hi, Nick," his dad said from the doorway.

Nick jumped. He thought the statue was talking to him.

"Hi, Dad," Nick said in a grumpy voice.

His dad walked into the room. He had on a suit he wore for work. He looked around. "You're cleaning up," his dad said. He picked up something from the floor and handed it to Nick.

It was a small wheel that belonged to a race car. Nick didn't know where the race car was.

"You have a lot of stuff in here," his dad said.

Nick didn't say anything. Whenever his dad brought up all of Nick's stuff he often followed it with a lecture about how thankful he should be or giving some of it to the poor.

His dad sat on the edge of the bed. "Your mom told me what happened," he said.

Nick saw the race car on a bookshelf. It only had three wheels. He picked it up and tried to put the missing wheel back on.

"Do you understand why it was wrong to go into our closet?" his dad asked.

Nick wanted to say "yes" so they wouldn't talk about it. His eye went to Saint Francis. *Saying "yes" would be a lie,* he thought.

"No," Nick said. "I don't get why it was wrong to look at our presents."

"Those aren't your presents," his dad said.

Nick looked at his dad. He was confused. "That's my RetroBlaster game. I saw it," he said.

"That game isn't yours until we give it to you," his dad said. "It belongs to us until then."

Nick hadn't thought of that. "But you will give it to me for my birthday, right?" he asked.

His dad stood up. He lifted up the bedcover. A paper plate was underneath. There was a piece of melted cheese stuck to it.

"This is why you're not supposed to bring food into your room," his dad said.

More rules, Nick thought. *I can't keep up with them all.*

"I hate to think of what else is buried in here," his dad said.

Nick thought about the half-eaten candy bar in the drawer.

"Do you think you should get a gift

after what you've done?" his father asked.

Nick didn't know what to say.

"I want you to think hard about why it was wrong to disobey us," his dad said.

"But you will give me the game for my birthday, right?" Nick asked.

His father gazed at him. "If you behave yourself and do everything your mom said, then maybe you'll have a nice birthday," his dad said.

"I will," Nick said.

His dad waved a hand at the room. "Do a thorough job on this bedroom," he said. "Clean out all the plates and food. Tidy your closet. And make sure to get everything out from under your bed."

"Okay, Dad," Nick said. He hoped this meant he would get the game for his birthday.

His dad walked out of the room carrying the paper plate.

Nick still wasn't sure that going into his parents' closet was such a bad thing. He knelt down and reached under the bed to get the baseball. He found his "Sponge Gun" there. It was a toy gun that shot little sponge balls. He had wondered where it was.

He used the gun to knock the baseball out from under the bed. A black sock was hooked to the gun. It was the match to the sock he found earlier.

He couldn't remember where he put the other sock. He rolled it up and shot it like a basketball at the laundry basket in the corner. He missed.

CHAPTER FIVE

▲▼◄▲▼◄▲▼◄▲▼◄▲▼◄▲▼◄

The Deep End

Samantha and her dad were at their local swimming pool. Sam was swimming while her dad read a book in one of the chairs on the side.

Mr. Perry put down his book. "It's time to go home!" he called out to Sam. He stood up and began to pick up their towels.

"Not yet," Sam called back. She wanted to keep swimming.

Mr. Perry pointed to the clock on the wall. "It's almost time for dinner," he said. Then he waved a hand to the rows of empty chairs. "You see? Everyone else has already gone. Even the lifeguard."

"But I don't want to go yet," Sam said. She had been enjoying being in the pool without a crowd of people around her.

Her father stopped and turned to her. His eyes were hidden behind his sunglasses. "We have been here for two hours," he said. "Don't spoil the time by arguing with me."

Sam sulked. "But we were late because you had errands," she complained. "You *always* have errands. And you talked for a long time to your office on the phone. Then you took forever getting ready."

"Two hours is better than nothing," her father said.

"Mom and I swim for *three* hours," Sam said. "Mom *always* spends more time with us than you do."

Sam knew she had hurt him. Her father stood still. He pressed his lips tightly together. She knew that meant he was trying to keep from being angry.

"Get your things," her father said in a low voice. He walked away through the gate.

Sam kicked at the water. She thought she could swim *one more* lap to the far end of the pool and back again. It wouldn't take long. Then she would leave.

She took a deep breath and dove into the water. She was a good swimmer. Her teacher said she was born to be in the water. She swam under the surface part of the way and then came up for air. She glanced around quickly. Her dad hadn't come back yet. She took another deep breath and pushed on. She was in the deep part now.

Suddenly she felt a sharp pain in her side. It was a cramp. It hurt a lot. She curled up for a second. Then she pushed up to the surface. At the top, she gasped for air. The sharp pain got worse. She went under again. She tried to kick to get to the side of the pool. The pain was worse when she stretched her legs out. She flailed at the water with her arms.

She reached the top and tried to cry for help. Her mouth filled with water. She went down again without getting a new breath. It felt like the water was pulling her down to the bottom. Her lungs burned. Black spots danced before her eyes. She wanted to breathe in so badly.

There is no one here to save me, she thought. *God, help me.*

Suddenly there was a burst of water next to her. Hands grabbed hold of her arms. She was pulled up and up. Then she was out of the water and being carried onto the cement.

She coughed and sputtered. The fresh air covered her skin and touched her face. With a few gasps she felt the air go into her lungs.

Sam looked up into the face of the one who had saved her. It was her dad. She began to cry.

Dad, she wanted to say.

He wrapped his arms around her and pulled her close.

A thought rushed through her mind. *I will remember this for the rest of my life.*

CHAPTER SIX

▲▼◀▲▼◀▲▼◀▲▼◀▲▼◀▲▼◀

Grace

It was a bright and sunny Saturday morning. A perfect day for the twins to celebrate their birthday.

Nick went into Sam's bedroom. She was sitting up in bed holding her ballerina. "You have to look really close to see where it broke," she said.

"At least you got a gift," Nick said. "I don't know if Mom and Dad will give me anything."

The Perry family moved to Hope Springs earlier in the summer. It was decided that the twins wouldn't have a big birthday party since they didn't have very many friends yet. Nick now worried about getting the RetroBlaster game he wanted. Sam had gotten the figurine of the ballerina. But she had asked for a Polly Playtime set.

"It's time for breakfast!" their mother called from downstairs.

Nick and Sam walked into the kitchen together.

"Surprise!" came the shout from Mr. Perry, Mrs. Perry, Andrew, and Lizzy. They stood around the kitchen table. It was decorated with streamers and balloons and birthday cards.

Sam put her hand to her mouth and giggled. Nick laughed.

"Sit down," their father said. He went to the stove and made their traditional birthday breakfast of pancakes.

Nick and Sam sat down and opened

their birthday cards. Some of them came from relatives around the country. A few of the cards had money inside.

Nick thought, *I'll have to use this money to buy a RetroBlaster game.* He was sure he wouldn't get the game as a gift today.

The pancakes were served and Mr. Perry told everyone to bow their heads. He made the Sign of the Cross and said, "Bless us, O Lord, and these thy gifts which we are about to receive…"

I hope I'm about to receive a gift, Nick thought.

"…from thy bounty, through Christ our Lord. Amen." "And thank you for the lives of Nick and Sam," he added.

"Amen," everyone said.

"Saint Clare of Assisi, pray for us," he said.

Nick remembered that their birthday was on the day the Church celebrated the life of Saint Clare.

"Let's go for a hike this morning," Mr. Perry said as they ate.

Nick and Sam both shouted, "Yay!"

Lizzy, their 10-year-old sister, wasn't the kind of person to shout "Yay!" She simply smiled.

Their 12-year-old brother Andrew said, "That'll be fun!" and took a big bite of his pancake.

"There's a special place I want you to see," their father said.

"What is it?" asked Andrew.

"You'll find out," their father said with a smile.

Mrs. Perry said, "Think about what you need for the hike. Get your backpacks ready."

When they were getting into the car later, Mrs. Perry looked at Sam's feet. Sam was wearing a new pair of sneakers they bought only a week ago.

"Those shoes aren't broken in. They will hurt your feet," her mom said.

Sam frowned. "But I love my new shoes," she said.

Nick struggled to put his backpack into the back of the car. It was heavy. Mr. Perry looked inside Nick's backpack. "Why are you bringing all this stuff?" he asked. "You won't need all these portable games."

"They're fun," Nick said.

"We're going on a hike," his dad reminded him. "You won't have time to play computer games."

"I'll play while we walk," Nick said.

Mr. Perry shook his head. "All right, let's go," he said.

They drove through Hope Springs to a mountain trail Nick had never seen before.

The Perry family began a nice walk up the mountain trail. The sky was blue. Birds sang all around them. Nick hardly noticed. He was playing on his portable game system.

"Look at the deer," Mrs. Perry said in a low voice.

Nick had just beat his highest score on the game. When he looked up the deer was gone.

The trail wound through the trees. They came to a steep hill. Sam began to limp. "My feet hurt," she whispered to Nick.

Nick's shoulders ached. His backpack was heavy. He felt thirsty. He reached for the water bottle in the side pocket of his backpack. It wasn't there. He had been so busy packing his games that he forgot about water. Then his game shut off. The power was gone.

Mr. and Mrs. Perry walked ahead with Andrew and Lizzy. They stopped to look at something.

Sam stopped and called out, "Wait!"

"What's wrong?" her dad called back.

Sam sat down on a large rock. "My feet hurt," she said.

Nick sat down next to her. He shook off his backpack. His shoulders were really sore.

The family gathered around Sam. Mrs. Perry knelt next to her and said, "Take off your shoes."

Sam obeyed. Her feet were red and becoming blistered.

Sam's parents looked at each other.

"Mom said you shouldn't wear those shoes," Andrew said. He was smiling at her.

Mrs. Perry reached into her backpack. She took out ointment and bandages. She put the ointment on all the red spots and wrapped Sam's feet with the bandage. Then she took out a pair of Sam's older hiking shoes.

"You brought them?" Sam asked.

Her mom nodded and carefully put them on Sam's feet.

"That's better," Sam said. "Thank you."

"Can I have a drink?" Nick asked. "I forgot my water bottle."

His dad let Nick drink from the water bottle he carried on his belt. The water tasted better than ever to Nick.

"It's a good thing Mom and Dad don't say 'I told you so,'" Lizzy said softly to the twins.

Their dad looked up. "Uh-oh," he said.

The sun disappeared behind a gathering of dark clouds.

The family walked further up the trail. A few drops of rain fell on them. Mr. and Mrs. Perry stopped to get the waterproof ponchos out of their backpacks. So did Andrew and Lizzy.

Nick and Sam looked at each other. They hadn't packed their ponchos. "Mom! Dad!" they called out.

CHAPTER SEVEN

▲▼◀▲▼◀▲▼◀▲▼◀▲▼◀▲▼◀

A Special Place

The rain didn't last very long. The Perry family huddled under some trees. The drops tapped the branches and leaves. Sam thought the browns and greens of the forest were beautiful.

Soon the tapping sound slowed down. Sam's dad stepped out from under the tree. "Let's go," he said.

They walked up the path through the woods. They climbed a small hill to a clearing. At the top the ground was flat and covered with tall brown weeds. In the middle of all the weeds stood a tall tower.

"What is that?" Sam asked.

"Is it part of a castle?" asked Nick.

"This is the special place," her father said. "It's not a tower. It's a chimney. We used to call this place Chimney Hill."

Mr. Perry led the family across the clearing.

"Why is there a chimney in the middle of nowhere?" Andrew asked.

Sam's foot kicked at something on the ground. She looked down. She could see cement mixed in with the dirt and weeds. *Was there a house here?* she wondered.

The family walked over to the chimney. It was built with fat gray stones. There was a large square hearth facing them. The hearth was full of rubble. They circled around to the other side. The back was solid.

They came around to the hearth again.

Mr. Perry reached into his backpack and took out some papers. One was a printout of an old and scratchy photo. In the photo was a large white house. It had two big doors on the front and a lot of windows upstairs and downstairs.

"The chimney was part of this house," Mr. Perry said.

In front of the house stood a family dressed in clothes people wore a long time ago. A man with a large mustache wore a top hat. A woman with her hair pinned up wore a frilly blouse and long skirt that was pinched tight around her waist. Four children stood around them. They looked like they were as old as Nick and Sam and younger. To the side a baby sat in a small basket on large wheels.

In the lower right-hand corner was handwritten "Paradise, 1902."

Lizzy pointed to the stone chimney in the picture. "It's the same chimney," she said.

"A rich family lived in this house over a hundred years ago," her father said. "But the house burned down. The chimney is all that's left."

"Was anybody hurt?" Sam asked.

"No," her father said. "The family had left before the house burned down."

"Why did it burn down?" Andrew asked.

"No one knows," Mr. Perry said.

Sam looked around. Once upon a time a happy family lived in a big pretty house here. Now it was gone. She felt sad.

"I used to play here when I was your age," Mr. Perry said.

Sam knew that her father grew

up in Hope Springs. His father and grandfather and great-grandfather and great-great-grandfather were well-known there. He left town to go to college. That's where he met their mother. His jobs kept him away from the town. But he always wanted to move back. They finally did earlier in the summer.

Nick went over to the hearth. He shrugged off his backpack and sat it down. He leaned in to try to look up the inside of the chimney. The rubble blocked his way.

"Watch out for snakes," Mrs. Perry said.

Sam shivered. She didn't like snakes.

"Did the chimney fall in?" Nick asked.

Mr. Perry shook his head. "The mayor had that filled in to keep kids from climbing inside," he said. "A boy got stuck up there and the fire department had to get him out."

"Were you the boy?" Mrs. Perry asked.

Mr. Perry laughed. "No. It was a kid at my school. Ethan Aaron," he said.

Lizzy moved away from the family and sat down on a large chunk of cement. She took a sketch pad from her backpack and began to draw. Sam walked around the field. She tried to imagine what kinds of rooms the house had and how the family lived back then. She looked back at the chimney. It looked so lonely standing there without a house nearby.

Nick went to the side of the chimney and began to test the stones. Then he reached up and grabbed a stone above his head. He put his foot on another stone and pulled himself up. Soon he was a foot off the ground.

"Be careful," Mrs. Perry called out. "You might fall."

Nick kept climbing higher. He was just above Andrew's head.

"I'm okay," Nick said. "Andrew will catch me," he said with a laugh.

Nick kept climbing higher. Sam was worried.

"That's far enough," Mr. Perry said.

Nick clung tightly to the stones and looked around. "It's a good view."

"What can you see?" Andrew asked.

"I see a construction site," Nick called out.

"That's where your Uncle Clark is building the new hotel," Nick's father said.

Nick turned his head and looked in another direction. "I wonder what that is," he said. He started to point but

nearly lost his balance.

Sam shrieked. She thought he was about to fall.

Nick grabbed the stones again. "Whoa!"

"Come down," Mrs. Perry said. She went to the base of the chimney and waited for him.

When Nick was back on the ground, Sam asked, "What did you see?"

"It looked like a run-down barn," Nick said. "Can we go look?" he asked.

"Not now," Mr. Perry said. "I have a surprise for you."

"What is it?" Nick asked.

His father put a hand on Nick's shoulder. "Follow me and you'll see."

The family walked away from the chimney.

Mrs. Perry suddenly stopped. "Aren't you forgetting something?" she asked Nick.

He looked at her, then at his

backpack still sitting next to the chimney. He groaned. "Does someone else want to carry it?" he asked. "My shoulders hurt."

No one offered.

Sam watched as Nick picked up the backpack.

"This isn't a very good day," he said as he walked past her.

CHAPTER EIGHT

▲▼◄▲▼◄▲▼◄▲▼◄▲▼◄▲▼◄

A Surprise

The Perry family left Chimney Hill and followed a path into the woods. Soon Nick could hear the sounds of trucks and men talking.

They came out of the woods to a large construction site.

"This is it," Mr. Perry said.

Just ahead was a tall chain-link fence with a sign that said "No trespassing." Beyond the fence men in orange jackets and hard hats were working. Bulldozers dug into the brown earth. Trucks carrying dirt drove away from them. Off to the side were trees that had been cut down.

Above the fence was a big sign that said, "A New Project from the Perry Company."

"Hey! That's our name," Sam said.

"It's your uncle's company," her father said. "He's building a big hotel. The biggest the town has ever seen."

"A *resort*," Mrs. Perry added. "It will have a huge swimming pool and golf course and even a place to ski further up the mountain."

Nick said, "Brad's dad says this will ruin nature. All the animals are being chased away."

Sam looked at the trees that had been knocked over. "Is that true?" she asked.

"Your uncle is doing his best to relocate the animals," Mr. Perry said. "He brought in experts to help. But some people will complain."

Nick remembered hearing Brad's father talk about getting the people in town to protest the building. Brad's father didn't want the town to ever change. But Nick knew his uncle was an important man and had big plans for how to help the town.

"This resort will help the town," Mrs. Perry said. "It will give people jobs and bring in a lot of visitors."

Sam pointed to a sign on another part of the fence. It said, "Beware of Bears and Other Wild Animals in the Area."

"Are there bears around here?" Sam asked.

Mrs. Perry knelt in front of Sam and tied her shoe. "We live in the Rocky Mountains," she said. "There may always be bears around."

"What are the rules if you happen upon a bear?" Mr. Perry asked them all.

"Don't run. Don't try to escape by

climbing a tree," said Andrew.

"Put your arms over your head to look bigger than you are," Lizzy said. "Don't provoke the bear or it might attack you."

"Keep eye contact and stay still," Sam said.

"Or back away slowly," Nick added.

"Good job," Mr. Perry said.

"There you are!" a deep voice called out from the other side of the fence.

A man walked toward them. He wore an orange vest with a business suit underneath.

"Uncle Clark!" Nick called out.

Uncle Clark was their dad's older brother. He reached the fence and said, "Happy birthday, Sam and Nick!"

Nick put his hands on the chain links. "Can we come in and look around?" he asked.

"You can do more than that," Uncle Clark said. He looked at his brother.

"Have you told them?"

"Not yet," Mr. Perry said. He turned to his family. "Uncle Clark is going to give you rides in the bulldozer," he said.

The kids gasped.

"Really?" Nick said. He was excited.

"For your birthday," Uncle Clark said. "Walk around the fence to the entrance."

The family followed the fence to a gate where Uncle Clark let them in to the construction site.

"Come to the office. You need to wear hard hats," he said.

They walked along a dirt path near the fence. Nick looked out to the woods. He could see the chimney sticking up from the trees. He wondered about the barn he'd seen when he climbed the chimney.

Big yellow diggers and trucks were busy going back and forth. Some roared loudly as they moved. Some made high beeping sounds.

The office was inside a long trailer. It had metal desks and chairs and filing cabinets. A couple of men worked at the desks. The office smelled like burnt coffee.

Uncle Clark handed out hard hats for them all to wear. "Give me a few minutes to arrange your ride," he said. Then he waved a hand to their dad. "First, I need your help with something."

"What's wrong?" Mr. Perry asked.

Uncle Clark waved for his brother to follow him. They stepped out of the trailer.

"Uh-oh," Mrs. Perry said. "There may be a problem."

Nick sat down on one of the metal chairs.

Mr. Perry came back in a minute later. "I'm sorry," he said. "There's something we have to take care of. It shouldn't take long."

Nick groaned. He knew what his dad was like when it came to his work. When he said "it shouldn't take long" that meant it would take longer than anyone thought.

"Can I take the kids outside?" Mrs. Perry asked. "They'll go crazy in here."

"Take them to see the Old Giant," Mr. Perry said.

"The Old Giant?" Sam asked.

Andrew smiled. "I remember the Old Giant," he said.

Nick imagined that they had an Old Giant helping to move the fallen trees. Like Paul Bunyan.

"Leave your backpacks here," Mrs. Perry said.

Nick was glad. He was very tired of carrying it around.

The family left the trailer and went behind it to a worn dirt path.

They walked alongside the chain-link
fence to an open grassy spot on the
construction site. In the middle of the
grass was a tractor run by steam.

"That's the Old Giant," Mrs. Perry
said. "Your uncle takes it to his
construction sites for good luck."

The tractor was painted mostly green
with red trim. But the paint had chipped
away to show the rust underneath. The
front was round and black with a tall
smokestack. It had large rear wheels
and smaller front wheels. A cab for the
driver sat between the wheels.

"I used to climb on this when we
came to visit," Andrew said. "Is it
okay?" he asked his mother.

She nodded.

Andrew climbed up into the cab.
Nick followed him. In the middle was a
metal chair. In front of the chair was a
steering wheel and levers.

"I wonder if it still runs," Andrew said.

Nick sat next to Andrew and tugged at one of the levers. It wouldn't move. "This is really old," Nick said.

"I think it's from the eighteen hundreds," Andrew said.

Sam climbed up to the cab. "Can I get in?"

"There isn't enough room," Nick said.

"I'll get out," Andrew said. He climbed down to let Sam in.

Sam sat down and reached for one of the levers.

"Don't touch that," Nick said.

"Why not?" Sam asked.

He frowned at her.

"Why are you in such a bad mood?" Sam asked softly.

"I want my RetroBlaster game," Nick said. "I think they're doing all this stuff because they won't give it to me."

"Maybe they will later," Sam said.

Nick shook his head. His sister didn't understand. He looked down at his mother. She was sitting with Lizzy on the grass. Lizzy had taken her sketch pad out. She was probably drawing the Old Giant.

Andrew had walked over to the edge of the site and was talking to one of the workers.

I'm bored, he thought. *I want to go home.*

He looked at the chain-link fence. In the distance he saw the chimney sticking up above the trees. He thought of the old barn he had seen. He stood up in the cab and tried to find where it was.

"What are you doing?" Sam asked.

"There!" Nick said. "I can see the old barn in the woods."

"So?" said Sam.

"I want to see what it is," Nick said.

"You just said what it is. It's an old barn," Sam said.

"What if it's more than that?" Nick asked. He jumped down from the tractor and went to the chain-link fence.

"Where are you going?" his mother asked.

"Just over here," Nick called back. He followed the chain-link fence in the direction of the barn.

"Slow down," Sam said behind him.

"Don't follow me," Nick said. "I want to do this by myself!"

"Do what?" Sam asked.

They were now behind another trailer. It blocked the view of the Old Giant and his mother.

"We should go back," Sam said.

"Why?" Nick asked. "Dad is going to take *ages* doing his work. I want to see the barn."

He kept walking. Sam kept following him.

Nick could see the barn more clearly now. "It's right over there," he said. "Through those trees."

Sam craned her neck to look.

The barn was a wooden building. From here Nick could see that the slats of wood were broken. There were big gaps in the sides.

On one end Nick saw something black and shiny. Then he saw something silver flicker in a shaft of sunlight.

"It's a car!" Nick said. He pushed along the fence to get a better view.

"You're going too far," Sam said.

Nick's sneaker caught on the bottom of the fence. He looked down. The chain-links had come away from the metal post. There was a gap he could crawl through. He knelt down.

"Nick," Sam said. "What are you doing?"

"I just want to run over to look," he said. He began to crawl through the gap in the fence.

"You *can't*," Sam pleaded.

"It'll only take a minute," Nick said. He was now on the other side of the fence.

"You should ask Mom," said Sam.

"Go tell Mom if you want," Nick said as he moved away. "I'll be back before she can say no."

Nick looked around. A trailer and a parked truck blocked the view of the old tractor. He imagined his mother sitting somewhere over there with Lizzy. He didn't look back as he ran across the field to the woods.

CHAPTER NINE

▲▼◄▲▼◄▲▼◄▲▼◄▲▼◄▲▼◄

The Car

Sam crawled through the fence to follow Nick. She wanted to tell her mom that he had left but knew it would make him mad. She thought she could keep him out of trouble if she went with him.

The old barn was broken down. She could see through the wooden slats on the side to something big and black inside. It was a car, like Nick said. There was a window with the glass busted out. Through it she could see the hood of the car.

"Is it a garage?" Sam asked.

Nick turned to her. "What are you doing here? Go back."

"Only if you will," she said.

"I will in a minute," he said.

They walked around to the front where two big wooden doors hung lopsided from broken hinges. Inside was an old-fashioned car. It was all black with spaces where the windshield and windows had been shattered. The body of the car was dented and rusted. The roof was bent in as if something heavy had been dropped on it. The front lights were round like eyes, but the glass had been smashed. The front tires were shredded and the rims sat on the ground.

Nick walked inside the barn. "Hey! Look at this," he said.

Sam followed him in. The barn was tall with rafters. There was a large bird's nest in the corner. Along the back were shelves with broken jars

and rusted cans. A thin ribbon of tire hung from a hook.

Nick pointed to the car. The black metal of the front and back doors were covered with small round holes that were now rusted.

Sam looked at the wall on that side of the garage. It was riddled with holes, too.

"Bullet holes!" Nick said.

"Vandals," Sam guessed out loud.

"Or maybe this was a hideout for gangsters and the police caught them," Nick said. His eyes were bright from the thought. "They had a shootout here."

"Okay, let's go now," Sam said. She was getting worried.

"Don't nag me," Nick said. He yanked at the front passenger door. It groaned loudly but didn't move. He pulled harder. It wouldn't budge. He glanced around and saw a cement block. He dragged it over to the side of the car and used it as a step to look in.

"Wow," he said.

Sam looked back at the construction site. She thought her mom might be standing at the fence looking for them. No one was there.

Sam jumped up on the block next to Nick. "Move over," she said.

The inside of the car was a mess. The cloth seats were ripped apart and springs stuck up every which way. The dashboard was busted up. There were large gaps where equipment had been stolen. The steering wheel hung down against the driver's seat.

Nick said, "I wonder what kind of car it is."

The ruined car and the thought of gangsters and bullet holes made Sam nervous. "I don't like it here," she said.

Just then there was a soft *snap* from somewhere outside.

"What was that?" Sam asked.

Nick stepped down from the block. There was another sound outside. He crouched down to look through the broken slats of wood. He gasped and stumbled backward.

Sam jumped down from the block. "What is it?" she asked. Her heart was pounding. "Is it a *bear*?"

"Worse than that," Nick said in a whisper.

"What could be worse?" Sam asked as she knelt to see what Nick was looking at. She put a hand to her mouth. Coming up along the garage was an animal with black fur and a white stripe down the back.

A skunk! Sam thought.

It was headed straight for the open doors.

Then she saw something following behind the large skunk.

"It's not *one* skunk," Sam said. "It's a *family* of skunks!"

CHAPTER TEN

AV◄AV◄AV◄AV◄AV◄AV◄

Trapped!

The twins backed up against the car. Sam remembered her dad telling a story about being sprayed by a skunk. He smelled bad for a week.

"What can we do?" Sam asked. The skunks were near the open doors. Sam counted seven baby skunks all moving together. They sniffed around the wood and floor of the barn.

"Dad told us what to do about bears," Nick said. "But he never said anything about skunks."

Nick grabbed a stone from the ground. "Let's throw stones to scare them away," he said.

"No! We might hurt one of them," Sam said.

"Maybe we can crawl out that way," Nick said. He pointed to the window on the side of the barn.

Just as he said it, a couple of the skunks disappeared around that side. The mother skunk came to the front of the car. She looked up at them and reared back with her front paws clawing at the ground. Her tail shot up into the air.

Sam backed up and bumped into

Nick. He was backing up from the other direction. Two of the skunks were at the rear of the car. Their tails were up in the air now.

"Go away!" Nick shouted. The baby skunks pawed at the ground just like their mother.

"Maybe we can climb up in the rafters," Sam said with a shaky voice.

Nick looked up. "The wood is rotten. We might fall," he said.

Sam looked at the car. "Let's hide in there. If we kneel down on the floor then they can't get us."

Nick nodded. He jumped onto the cement block and checked the window for any broken glass. "No glass," he said. He climbed into the car.

Sam got onto the block. The large skunk had turned its rear around to them. The little skunks were doing the same thing. Sam scrambled in next to Nick.

The front seat was such a mess that they had to crawl into the back. There was space between the front seats and back seats for them to crouch down low.

"We never should have come here," Sam said.

"I told you to stay back," Nick said.

They pressed in close together. Sam could hear Nick's breathing, short and fast. They didn't dare get up to look. All they could do was listen.

Soon they could hear the skunks walking and scratching outside of the car. The skunks made high-pitched squeaking sounds.

"Why don't they go away?" Sam asked. "It stinks in here."

"It'll be worse out there," Nick said. He got up to look out the windows on both sides of the car. "We're surrounded," he said.

"What are they doing?" Sam asked.

"Sniffing around. Watching us. Some of them are under the back of the car," Nick said.

Sam's eye caught something move in the corner of the back seat. Her body tensed when she saw a large hole. A black nose poked through.

She froze. "They're in the trunk," Sam whispered.

Nick spun around.

"This is their home!" Sam said, realizing why they wouldn't go away. "They made a nest in the trunk!"

The twins looked at each other. How were they going to get out of this?

"Crawl through the window and get on the roof," Nick said. He reached up to the driver's side window. Sam did the same on the passenger side.

The skunks seemed to be everywhere below them.

The twins were on the roof. It made a bang and dropped a few inches.

"It's going to cave in!" Nick said. "Let's jump on the hood and run through the doors," he said.

"What if the hood won't hold us?" Sam asked.

"Do you have a better plan?" Nick asked.

Sam didn't. "Okay."

She crouched onto the roof of the car. Then she slowly stood up. She balanced herself.

"Hurry up," Nick said. "If we get back fast Mom won't know we were here."

Sam gathered her strength. She then leapt from the roof to the hood. The hood gave a loud bang. Sam nearly lost her balance but sprung forward toward the open doors of the barn. She hit the dirt and rolled. She got to her feet. She was in the clear.

The skunks were rushing around the car. They squealed loudly. Their tails were in the air.

Sam saw one of the baby skunks crawl up onto the seat of the car.

"Come on!" Sam shouted.

Nick now stood up on the roof. It made a loud crunching sound. He leapt onto the hood of the car. It suddenly buckled. Nick's feet slipped in one direction while his arms pinwheeled in the other direction. He fell from the car onto the side. The skunks screeched at him.

Sam took a few steps toward the barn to help Nick.

He leapt up and shouted, "No! No! They're spraying me!"

Sam could smell it already. It was a stink unlike any stink she had ever smelled before.

Nick stumbled out of the garage. He brushed at his clothes and kicked his legs as if trying to shake off the skunk spray.

From somewhere through the trees

Sam heard her mom shout, "Nick! Sam! Where are you?"

Chapter Eleven

▲▼◀▲▼◀▲▼◀▲▼◀▲▼◀▲▼◀

No Escape

Nick did not get a ride in the tractor. His Uncle Clark didn't want the equipment to smell like skunk. Instead Mr. Perry poured water in Nick's eyes to make sure none of the skunk spray had hurt him there. Then Nick was wrapped up in an old tarp and put in a pickup truck.

One of Uncle Clark's men drove Nick and Mrs. Perry back to the house. Nick's mom said she had a special mix to help get rid of the smell.

They drove with the windows down.

Uncle Clark's man was named Bob. He laughed the whole way and kept wiping his eyes.

At home Nick saw his mom pull out a box marked "Baking Soda" and a bottle of vinegar and a brown bottle with really long words on it. She mixed it all in a bucket with some water and put Nick's clothes in. She used a broom handle to push it down over and over.

"Now it's your turn," she said to Nick. She was not happy with him.

She mixed everything together in another bucket and took him out to the middle of their garage. She made him stand still while she scrubbed him down from head to toe.

"Ouch," he said. It felt like she was rubbing his skin off.

"We may have to do this a few times," she said. "Now be still. We have to leave it on your skin for five minutes."

She gave him an old towel to wrap around his waist.

"What were you thinking?" Mrs. Perry asked Nick.

He lowered his head. "I wanted to see the barn," he said.

"You know you should have asked," his mom said. "You could have wandered off, gotten lost, or been hurt worse than this. How would we have known?"

"Sam was with me," Nick said.

Mrs. Perry gazed at him. "She's in trouble, too. But I'm going to guess that she went because she was worried about you. Am I right?"

Nick nodded.

"First the closet and now this," Mrs. Perry said with a frown. "What are we supposed to do? It's your birthday. We wanted this to be a good day for you."

Nick didn't say anything.

"Wait here while I get another washcloth," she said. She walked out of the garage.

I'll never get that RetroBlaster game now, he thought.

Later, the rest of the family came home. They were excited about riding in a tractor and a digger, and Andrew had even held on to a jackhammer.

Nick listened to them with a stiff smile on his face.

Mr. Perry told them why he had

been called away by Uncle Clark. A digger on the construction site found old artifacts.

"What are artifacts?" Sam asked.

"Things left behind by people who died a long time ago," Mr. Perry said. "They looked like old Native American pots and plates. Some looked Spanish. They may be artifacts from Spanish missionaries."

"What will Clark do?" Mrs. Perry asked.

"Bring in experts," Mr. Perry replied.

Nick sat on the couch and sulked. Everything fun happened while he was home getting skunk smell scrubbed off of him.

"I can hardly smell the skunk," Sam said to Nick.

He grunted at her. "Mom had to wash me three times," he said.

Sam looked at him as if she wanted

to say something else. Then she turned and walked away.

"What are we going to do with you?" Mr. Perry asked Nick after the others had gone off to other parts of the house.

"I don't smell like skunk now," Nick said. He sniffed at his arm and wrinkled his nose. "Maybe a little."

His dad sat down next to him on the couch. "I hope you're getting the lesson," he said.

This is one of those things parents say as a trick, Nick thought. *If I say I got the lesson then I'll have to say what the lesson was. If I say I don't then I'll get a long lecture.* He didn't know what to say.

"You disobeyed us by going into the closet," his dad said. "Now it's your birthday, and you're not sure whether or not we'll give you that game you wanted."

Nick looked at his dad like he was a

mind-reader.

"You've been sulking all day," his dad continued. "You put too much stuff in your backpack. You weren't prepared for the hike. And you suffered for it."

Nick slowly nodded.

Mr. Perry leaned forward. "You wandered off without permission because you wanted to see that barn. You thought you could sneak off by yourself and sneak back again. Am I right?"

Nick said "yes" very softly.

"You might have gotten away with it. But then you got sprayed by that skunk," his dad said. "God may have been watching over you."

"How?" Nick asked. He couldn't think of anything worse than being sprayed by that skunk.

"A family of bears was seen in the area, too," his dad said.

Nick shuddered. What if he had bumped into the bears instead of the skunks?

"There are reasons why we let you do some things and why we won't let you do other things," his dad said. "I would have taken you to see that barn, if you had waited. But you didn't. You were pouting and angry. Your impatience got you in trouble in the closet. Do you see how your feelings have given you a bad birthday?"

"A bad *week*," Nick said. He couldn't argue with anything his father was saying. He felt stupid now. And feeling stupid made him feel sorry for himself.

"You're suffering because of the choices you made," Mr. Perry said. "That's the lesson you have to learn."

"Does that mean I won't get a birthday present?" Nick asked.

His father patted him on the knee.

"We'll talk about that at dinner," he said.

Nick didn't know if that should give him hope or not.

▲▼◀▲▼◀▲▼◀▲▼◀▲▼◀▲▼◀

CHAPTER TWELVE

The End of the Day

Mr. and Mrs. Perry fixed a celebratory dinner of pepperoni pizza with extra cheese. It was the twins' favorite. Mr. Perry prayed before they ate and thanked God for Nick and Sam.

But there were no presents. Mrs. Perry brought out a large plate of ice cream cupcakes made with vanilla and chocolate. A candle was put in one for Sam and another candle in another for Nick. They sang "Happy Birthday," and the twins blew out the candles.

Nick wished he would get the RetroBlaster game.

The family ate their cupcakes and went into the family room to play games. Nick looked over at Sam. She seemed to be having a lot of fun.

Nick kept thinking his parents would suddenly bring out their presents. But they didn't.

Then it was time for bed.

Nick put on his pajamas. He went into the bathroom to brush his teeth. *They aren't going to give me my present*, Nick thought. He fumed. It was his birthday. It shouldn't matter what he did wrong.

Nick went into Sam's room. She stood in her pajamas and was putting her ballerina on her nightstand.

"I'm glad *somebody* got a present today," Nick said.

Sam looked at him. "Did you ever say you were sorry?" she asked.

Nick had to think. Did he ever say he was sorry? He wasn't sure. "I think so," he said.

"Did you ask for forgiveness?" Sam asked.

Nick rolled his eyes. "What's the difference?" he asked.

"You say you're sorry when you've done something wrong by accident," Sam said. "You ask for forgiveness when you've done something wrong on purpose."

Nick groaned. "Why does it have to be so hard?" he asked.

Sam pressed her lips together and glared at him. "*You* made it hard," she said. Nick snorted and walked out. He went to his room and looked around. He hoped his parents had sneaked his present onto his bed while he was brushing his teeth. No present was there.

He sat on the bed and pouted.

His dad came in and sat on the bed next to him. "Tough day," he said.

"Yeah," said Nick. He looked up at his dad. "I'm not going to get my present today, am I?"

"Do you think you should?" his dad asked.

It felt like another trick question. Nick sighed.

"The funny thing about gifts is that we don't deserve them," his dad said. "That's what makes them different from a reward or payment."

Nick said, "I know that."

His dad turned on the bed to face Nick. "Gifts are one of the ways we show you that we love you. But we still love you even if we don't give you gifts."

Nick frowned. *Does that mean I won't get a gift?* he wondered.

"Would it be wrong to give you a gift when you've disobeyed?" his dad asked.

"No," Nick said and knew he answered too quickly.

"No?" His dad tilted his head a little. "Then you might think we're rewarding you for disobeying us."

"I won't think that," Nick said. "I'm sorry."

His dad gave him a small smile. "Are you? I'm not so sure." His dad stood up. "You may have to do something to prove that."

"Like what?" Nick asked.

"You were supposed to do a good

job cleaning your room," his dad said.

"I tried," Nick said. The room looked clean to him.

His dad walked around the room. "Maybe you should try harder. It doesn't look like you cleaned under the bed."

Nick frowned again. *I have to do chores on my birthday?* he thought sadly.

His dad seemed to know what he was thinking. "Did you mean it when you said you were sorry?"

"Yes," Nick said.

His dad gave him an amused look. Then he held out his arms. Nick slid off the bed and slowly went to him.

His dad pulled him close. "I'm glad you're my son," he said.

They hugged. Then Nick felt another pair of arms come around him.

"Me too," his mom said. "Happy birthday."

His mom brushed her fingers through his hair. "I hope you sleep well," she said.

His parents went out of his room and pulled the door until it was open only a crack. Nick crawled into bed and pushed under his covers. He didn't want to clean under his bed now. He didn't want to do anything. He just had the worst birthday ever. All he wanted to do was go to sleep.

He fell back onto his pillow. *How can I sleep?* he asked himself. He sat up again. *This is terrible.*

He kicked at the covers. He swung his legs off of his bed and sat for a minute.

My room doesn't look so bad.

He couldn't remember if he had cleaned under his bed. He thought he had. He dropped down onto the floor and crouched to look. There was nothing there.

I cleaned under my bed, he thought.

Then he saw a box in the dark shadows under the headboard against the wall. He almost missed it. He groaned. How did his dad know he'd missed this one thing?

He half-crawled under the bed and pulled at the box. It was heavy. He couldn't think what it might be. Probably some old stuff he never played with. He tugged at the box and got it into the light. It was plain cardboard with no writing on it at all.

He lifted the lid. Inside was a brand new RetroBlaster game.

"What?" he said out loud.

Suddenly there was a burst of laughter from the door. His father and mother stood there with Andrew, Lizzy, and Sam. Sam was holding a Polly Playtime doll.

"Happy birthday!" they shouted.

Chapter Thirteen

AV◄AV◄AV◄AV◄AV◄AV◄

The High Road

Nick and Sam spent the week after their birthday enjoying their presents. Sam played with her Polly Playtime Doll. Nick and his friend Brad worked to get to new levels on the RetroBlaster game.

Then Friday came. Friday was the day Nick and Sam were given money by their parents for the chores they did during the week. This week was special because Nick and Sam got extra money from relatives for their birthday.

Both kids put half of the money into small piggy banks they kept in their rooms. Sam's bank looked like a music box. Nick's bank was shaped like a football.

That morning, Brad asked them why they put half their money in the piggy banks.

"To save for things we want to buy later," Nick said.

"We are saving up for bikes," Sam said. "I want a dark red Wing-Flyte bike."

Nick said, "I want a Special Edition High Road mountain bike."

Brad's eyes lit up. "My older brother is selling that bike."

Nick was surprised. "Why is he selling it?" he asked.

"He outgrew it," Brad said. "You should buy his."

Nick was excited by the idea.

"Mom and Dad won't let you buy a bike they haven't seen," said Sam.

"But it's your money," Brad said. "You should be able to buy whatever you want with it."

Brad is right, Nick thought.

"You should wait until Dad gets home," Sam said.

Brad said, "You can wait. But I think my brother has someone else who wants to buy it today."

Later Nick told his mother about Brad's brother and the High Road bike for sale.

"I know how much you want that bike," she said. "But you have to wait until your father comes home."

"But it's *my* money," Nick said.

"Wait," Mrs. Perry said firmly.

Nick went up to his room. He paced around and kept looking at his bank. *It's my money,* Nick thought.

He picked up his bank and sat down on the floor. The money rattled inside. He took the plug from the bottom and shook everything out onto the carpet. There were a lot of dollars and coins. He slowly counted it all. He had $97.32. It was a lot more than he thought.

He wondered how much Brad's brother was asking for the bike.

What if he sells it before I get there? Nick thought.

Nick shoved the money into his pockets.

He went downstairs to the front door. "I'm going out to play," he called out to his mom. He didn't wait to hear her answer.

He went into the backyard and kicked a soccer ball around for a little while.

Sam came out and asked if he wanted to play.

"No," he said. "I'm going to take a walk."

Sam knew her brother well. "Don't go to Brad's," she said.

"Why would I do that?" Nick asked and walked away.

He thought about the High Road mountain bike. He put his hands in his pockets. His fingers touched the money.

"It's my money," he said to himself.

Brad lived only two streets away.

Chapter Fourteen

▲▼◄▲▼◄▲▼◄▲▼◄▲▼◄▲▼◄

The Low Road

Nick knocked on the front door of Brad's house.

Brad answered the door. He smiled at Nick. "Luke is in the garage," he said.

Luke was Brad's 14-year-old brother. A lot of the kids in the neighborhood thought he was cool.

Brad led Nick through the house and out into the garage. The garage looked like an explosion at a car mechanic's shop. Shelves were filled with parts of machinery and boxes.

Luke stood at a workbench with a screwdriver in his hand.

"This is Nick," Brad said.

Luke didn't turn to look at Brad. Instead he pointed to the corner of the garage. "There it is," he said.

Nick's heart jumped. A Special Edition High Road mountain bike leaned against the wall. Nick walked over to it.

The bike was splattered with mud. The paint had a few dings and scratches.

"Does it work?" Nick asked.

"Yep," said Luke. "Just like new."

Nick felt the tires. They were filled with air. "How much does it cost?" Nick asked.

"How much do you have?" Luke asked.

"$97," Nick said.

Luke shrugged. "I'll sell it to you for $97."

Nick looked at the bike again.

"Can I take it for a ride?" Nick asked.

"Sure. But make up your mind fast," Luke said. "I have someone else who wants to buy it."

Nick pulled the bike away from the wall and began to turn it around. Then his eye went to a shelf next to the bike. He saw a RetroBlaster System One with game cartridges sitting in a box.

"Wow!" he shouted.

Brad chuckled. "I thought you would notice that," he said.

Luke looked over at them. "I'm selling everything on that shelf," he said.

Nick leaned the bike against the wall again. He went to the shelf. The RetroBlaster System One looked like new. The game cartridges were still in their original cases. Then he saw some of the other boxes. In one was a set of

Super Spy Night Goggles. Another box had a small battery-powered remote-control helicopter. Another box had a Fast-Changer Robot that turned from a car into a battleship.

Nick wanted them all.

Brad laughed at him. "You came for the bike," he said.

Luke saw Nick's expression. He said, "You can take them all home for $90."

Nick looked at the bike. He looked at the boxes. $97 for one bike. $90 for all of this cool stuff. What should he do?

Nick pulled the money out of his pocket. If he bought the boxes, he would still have $7 left over. "I want what's on the shelf," Nick said. He gave the money to Luke.

What a deal! he thought.

Brad said he would help carry the boxes back to Nick's house.

The two boys walked along the sidewalk. Nick was thrilled. It was like having another birthday.

They passed Damian's Corner Store.

"I'm thirsty," Brad said. "You should buy me a drink since I'm helping you."

Nick said okay. They went inside and Nick bought a drink for Brad and a drink for himself. He bought snacks they both liked. By the time he paid for it all, he had only six cents left.

The two boys sat at a picnic table next to the store.

"I can't wait to see the look on your dad's face when he sees all this," Brad said.

Nick felt his blood run cold. His mom had said not to buy anything until his dad came home. Now he was going to walk in with all these boxes.

Nick thought about it. "I want to hide everything in my room and surprise him later," he said.

Brad finished his drink and snack. He looked at a clock on the wall and cried out, "Oh no! I'm late for practice! I have to go home!"

"You can't leave me!" Nick said.

"I can't be late!" Brad said and ran off.

Nick sighed. It was going to be hard carrying those boxes home.

And it was. The boxes were heavy. And they got heavier as he walked. They reminded him of his heavy backpack when he went on that hike with his family.

He thought how easy it would have been to ride the bike home.

Just then his foot caught on an uneven part of the sidewalk. He tripped. Everything in his arms flew away. The RetroBlaster game crashed onto the hard cement and shattered.

"No!" Nick shouted.

Nick slowly picked everything up. One of the rotors on the helicopter was bent. The Spy Goggles' glass was broken. The Quick-Change Robot was in small pieces.

Nick sat down. He felt like crying. What would his parents say?

CHAPTER FIFTEEN

▲▼◄▲▼◄▲▼◄▲▼◄▲▼◄▲▼◄

The Long Road

Nick sat on the sidewalk and looked
at all the things he had bought.
They were now broken or ruined. He
looked in the direction of his house. It
seemed far away.

He felt stupid. How could he go
home now?

He wondered if Luke would give
him his money back.

No, he thought. Luke wouldn't give
him money for boxes of broken stuff.

Nick sat down on the curb. He

thought about how he had sneaked into his parents' closet to look at the birthday gifts. He thought about all the trouble he had on his birthday. He got sprayed by a skunk. He had disobeyed his parents over and over. Now he had spent all his money after his mom told him not to. What was he going to do?

Mom and Dad will be so angry, he thought. He put his head in his hands. "Saying I'm sorry won't be good enough," he said to an ant crawling along the curb below him.

He had never thought about running away before. Now he began to think it was a good idea.

There is an old shed in the woods, he thought. *Maybe I could live there.*

He lifted his head and looked at the boxes. They looked like nothing but junk now.

Nick couldn't go home. Not until he could think of something to say.

He stood up and slowly picked up the boxes. He turned away from home and walked back toward the corner store. There was a path that cut through the houses into the woods. He followed the ruts deep into the trees. Off to the side was the old shed he and Sam had found one day. Someone said it was over a hundred years old. No one used it now.

Nick pushed the door open with his foot. There was nothing in the shed except a spiderweb in the corner. He put the boxes down on the dirt floor. He sat down. He wanted to cry.

He felt so tired. All of that walking with those heavy boxes was hard.

He lay down and rested his head on his arm. He just needed a moment to think of what to do.

Soon he fell asleep.

He dreamed that his father and mother were outside calling for him.

He woke up to the feeling of something wet hitting his face. He sat up. It was raining outside. The roof of the shed had long cracks in it. Rain dripped down inside. A puddle had formed next to where Nick lay.

Nick felt cold. It was getting dark outside. His stomach growled. It must be close to dinner time. Maybe past it. More water dropped on his head. He knew he couldn't stay here.

He slowly gathered up his boxes of

junk. He felt sad as he thought about his mom and dad. He wondered if they would feel sorry for him. Maybe they wouldn't punish him too much.

They will, he thought. *I've done a lot of things wrong lately.*

He wondered why he acted the way he did.

He came out of the woods. The rain fell on him. He walked past the corner store to his street. He looked down at the sidewalk. He saw a large puddle and took a step to miss it. His foot went into a small hole. The boxes fell out of his hands like they had before. One of them splashed into the puddle. The other spilled onto the grass.

Nick looked down at the soaked boxes. He began to cry.

"Son," a voice said.

Nick looked up. A car had pulled up next to the curb. The lights were on and the windshield wipers scraped back and forth. Nick's dad stood by the open driver's door.

"I've been looking for you," his dad said softly. "I even called Brad's house."

Nick looked at the junk on the ground and then back at his father.

"Do you need some help?" his dad asked.

Nick wiped at the water on his face. "I'm sorry," he said.

His dad knelt down. Together they put the junk back into the boxes.

"I'm sorry," Nick said again. "I'm sorry for sneaking into your closet and going to that barn and spending my money and being so bad. I'm sorry. Please forgive me."

His dad was by his side. He felt his father's arms around him.

"Let's go home," his father said.

CHAPTER SIXTEEN

▲▼◄▲▼◄▲▼◄▲▼◄▲▼◄▲▼◄

Home Again

Sam walked into Nick's bedroom. She carried a large blow-dryer in her hands.

Nick was in his pajamas sitting on his bed. He was looking at the palms of his hands. He had scraped them on the sidewalk when he fell. His mom made him take a hot bath when he got home. She was afraid he might catch a cold from being in the rain.

All of the things Nick bought from Brad's brother were spread out on the bedroom floor. Sam plugged in the

blow-dryer.

"What are you doing?" Nick asked.

"Dad told me to use this to dry off your stuff," Sam said. She turned on the blow-dryer. It made a loud roar as the warm air blasted out. She felt it push back in her hand.

She pointed the air at the RetroBlaster game console. A corner of the plastic was chipped off. There was a long crack along the top. The front display had a spiderweb break in it.

Nick came over to Sam. He watched her blast the blow-dryer for a moment.

"Did Mom and Dad give you a big lecture?" Sam asked.

Nick shook his head. "They didn't say anything. They've been really nice."

"We were worried," Sam said. "All of us went out looking for you. Mom even went back to Chimney Hill."

"Why would I go back to Chimney Hill?" he asked.

"We didn't know what you were thinking," Sam said.

Nick didn't say anything.

Sam thought he looked tired. She also thought he still smelled a little bit like skunk spray.

"Do you think Dad can save any of this stuff?" Sam asked him.

Nick knelt down and spread out some of the RetroBlaster game cartridges. "Dad says we'll fix what we can," he said. "We'll make it our special project over the next week."

"What if you can't fix any of it?" Sam asked.

"Then I guess we'll throw everything away." Nick picked up the Spy Goggles. They were shattered. "These go first." He tossed them into the trash basket.

Sam felt sorry for Nick. He'd spent

all of his money and didn't even get what he really wanted. It would take a long time to earn that money again.

She turned a little to blow air on another part of the RetroBlaster. She saw a flicker of light on the floor. A quarter sat next to the leg of a dresser.

"Look," she said and pointed.

Nick picked up the quarter. He dropped the quarter into his football bank. It made a loud *chink* sound. "I'll have to start over."

Sam thought about all the things they had done wrong over the past week and how they were allowed to start over. The words "love" and "forgiveness" stuck in her head.

She kept the blow-dryer on the game system while Nick looked over the game cartridges.

"I don't even like most of these games," he said sadly.

Sam hoped Nick had learned a lesson. She hoped life at home would calm down now.

Mrs. Perry peeked in the door. "Time to get ready for bed," she said to Sam.

Sam looked at the clock on Nick's nightstand. It said 8:00. "It's early," Sam said.

"You need to get used to going to bed early," her mom said.

"Why?" Nick asked.

"Because you'll be getting up earlier," Mrs. Perry said.

The twins looked at each other, confused.

"School starts in a week," their mom said.

Sam and Nick looked at each other. Their eyes grew wide with alarm.

"School!" they shouted. "Oh no!"